BLACK MARKER

BLACK MARKER

A NOVEL IN 100-WORD STORIES

RAN WALKER

Cover image used courtesy of Asher Legg

Additional images used courtesy of
Yingchou Han, Alexander Andrews, Janko Ferlič,
Gaman Alice, and Mike Von

ISBN: 9781020001345
Library of Congress Control Number: 2022910931
First Edition

Black & Square
An Imprint of 45 Alternate Press, LLC
Hampton, VA

In memory of Dr. Bruce Cole,
who supported me from the very beginning

CONTENTS

PREFACE

This is the kind of book that screams for a preface, something to contextualize what you're about to read. The last time I wrote a book like this was when I penned *Work-In-Progress* back in 2018. That was the kind of book only its author could love. In a genre where there's not a ton of avant-garde writing, *Work-In-Progress* was the first step I took where I lost a number of my previous fans because I had deliberately "jumped the shark" on African-American fiction.

Thankfully, there have been a number of books since then that have embraced Afrosurrealism. Still, playing with this genre using microfiction is not only unusual, it takes something that is already strange and puts it into an even stranger form. But this is where I am creatively—at least right now.

I see *Black Marker* as a combination of two different Black television shows: *Woke* (Keith Knight's autobiographical comedy about race in the Bay Area) and *Atlanta* (Donald Glover's Afrosurrealistic escapades surrounding a Southern rapper and his close circle of friends). It also has touches of César Aira's *fuga hacia adelante* method of writing, which results in the plot changing and things shifting into entirely new things.

In short, this is the kind of book that was fun for me to write and one that I'm sure will push you, dear reader, into some interesting (and hopefully enjoyable) directions.

Be easy in the meantime, and thank you for taking this journey with me.

Ran Walker

June 2022

All things must change to something new,
to something strange.

HENRY WADSWORTH
LONGFELLOW

Comic
Sans

It took only one question for Gerald to know he'd probably made a mistake agreeing to speak to the students at MLK Middle School.

"So you do stuff like *SpongeBob SquarePants*?" one kid asked.

"I don't make cartoons."

"But you said you were a cartoonist," the kid replied.

"I do a comic strip about my life," Gerald said.

"So you're a comic stripper then!" the kid yelled, basking in the laughter of his classmates.

Gerald sighed. "I guess so. Just me and your mom, hanging out cracking jokes on the pole. By the way, tell her I said 'what's up?'"

HE KNEW he needed to work on his patience, but as he often pointed out to people, he was a work in progress.

"Still, you can't talk to children like that," the principal had warned him.

Gerald nodded his head, taking the reprimand. As long as they gave him his check.

It was no secret all of this would be drawn into three panels, giving that kid bragging rights for the rest of the sixth grade.

"We'd love to have you back. Just tone it down a little," the principal said, adding, "Feel free to use *this* in your strip."

3

EACH MORNING GERALD stood in front of the mirror and repeated to himself that he was a good cartoonist, that he wasn't wasting his life, that he hadn't actually missed his true calling elsewhere in his obsession to frame his life in panels.

From time to time he drew variations of this scene: him standing in front of the mirror, questioning his life. His fans seemed to enjoy his bouts with these existential crises.

It seemed as though the only thing they loved more were the scenes featuring his girlfriend, Tammi, scenes that were about to get even more interesting.

4

IF NOT FOR SYNDICATION, he wouldn't have had enough to buy a ring.

He'd had to be a bit of a sleuth to find out Tammi's ring size and the diamond cut. He'd even phoned her parents on the other side of the country to do the gentlemanly thing of asking for her hand.

He was ready.

After all, they'd been living together for two years and their life was good. This was what responsible grown folks did, he reasoned. It was time to take it to the next level.

He'd even drawn the panels already—everything except her reaction.

5

THE PLAN for the proposal was simple: they'd go out to dinner at her favorite spot, then take a walk along the promenade overlooking the ocean. He'd find a clean spot to kneel down, leaving the moon and stars as his backdrop, and then pop the question.

He wondered how she would react. Would she jump up and down like a Price Is Right contestant winning a car and cry, or would it be a more subdued "It's about damn time!"

Either way, the thought of being able to call Tammi his wife was a high in and of itself.

HE HADN'T ANTICIPATED her answer. He was too unaware of his obtuseness for that.

"I hate being a part of your work. You have no filter at all. I have people at work laughing at me behind my back because they read something you wrote about our personal life. I love you, but being in a relationship with you is exhausting," she'd said.

"So I take it's that's a 'no' then?" he'd answered.

"I think it's best we move on."

By the end of the week, she'd moved out of the apartment, whispering "hallelujah" under her breath the entire time.

GERALD HAD to rewrite the engagement panel, and when his mind stalled on him while approaching the deadline, he'd decided to just keep the panel illustrations exactly the same, including her excited reaction. He simply changed the "Yes!!!" to a "No!!!"

He looked at it through bleary eyes and allowed himself to chuckle at it, but the chuckle was short-lived.

With the last of his emotional and physical energy, he cleaned up the artwork and digitized it before sending the final file to Bob at Arroyo Syndication.

"You sure you want to do this?" Bob asked.

"Why not?" Gerald managed.

OVER THE WEEKEND, he buried himself beneath the covers on his bed, the blinds pulled tightly. He could still smell Tammi's fragrance in the fabric.

How could he have missed the signs? Did she tell *anyone* about her feelings? Her parents didn't seem to know.

What about the sex? Was she just going through the motions?

How long would they have been together if he had never proposed to her? Would she still be there, going through the motions?

They were beyond therapy, he guessed.

He kept wondering if he could've done anything differently—besides including her in his strip.

WHEN HE SAT down to write his weekly panels, his mind went blank. The black marker sat in his hands, feeling like some foreign object he'd discovered while scuba diving in the chasm of his own heart.

Three panels lay before him. In the past, his mind was eager to fill those spaces, and on good days, he laughed as he drew the scenes, imagining how his fans would respond to them.

Now he was empty. Even worse, he didn't have any idea of how to get back on track.

Tammi had been his muse. Now the well was dry.

THERE WAS a part of Gerald that missed Tammi the person, but then there was a part of him that missed Tammi the character. What was Garfield without Odie? Snoopy without Woodstock? Even when she wasn't in the strip, her energy was there.

He had hoped Bob would be understanding about his need for a hiatus.

"Buck the fuck up and be a professional," Bob had said. "We pay you to do a job. Dammit, do it!"

Maybe it was something in the water, but Gerald, unable to see past his own emotions, did one of Tammi's numbers.

"I'm out."

STARING into the mirror the following morning, he said, "I'm a cartoonist. I am a grown-ass cartoonist. I am a grown-ass, unemployed cartoonist."

He laughed as he said this (almost maniacally, if he'd allowed himself to consider it). If this was a strip, his fans would love it.

Fans?

What was a fan—really? (He could feel the existential crisis creeping up on him.)

And like that, he suddenly realized that, for the first time in the past three years, he was not performing or curating his life for anyone.

There was something oddly scary, yet liberating, about that idea.

"I QUIT MY JOB," he told Tammi over the phone.

"No one told you to do that."

"But that was the thing interfering with our re-lationship. I wanted to see if we could try again."

"It's not a good time for me."

"It's only been a week. Surely there are some feelings still there."

"Actually, I kind of met someone."

"Met someone? We just broke up!"

"Yeah. I wasn't looking for it to happen. It kinda just did."

Gerald swallowed. "Well, *fuck me*," he whis-pered under his breath.

"Not anymore," Tammi responded before hanging up.

The cartoon gods were laughing.

"What were you thinking?" Charlotte asked.

Gerald loved his big sister, but he sometimes resented her tough love, especially when it was doled out over the phone, from a different time zone.

"I panicked. I thought I could get Tammi back."

"Never, ever quit your job if you don't have another one lined up."

"Yeah, I know."

"Maybe you could go back to them and see if you can get your job back. You know they don't pay unemployment for people who quit."

He knew she was right.

He'd definitely have to grovel—and he wasn't too proud for that.

GERALD KISSED ASS, as only a desperate man could, but Bob was unmoved, his ass apparently unfazed by the robust affection of tender lips.

There'd be no additional strips for *Broken Bicycle* (he had always hated that name!), and the cartoon was destined to embrace a fate not unlike that of a beloved Black sitcom: no true finale.

The world (or at least the 250 newspapers that ran the cartoon) would know *Broken Bicycle* as that strip that ended with the guy getting rejected after proposing to his girlfriend.

It was sadly ironic, damn near perfect when Gerald considered it.

IT WOULDN'T HAVE MATTERED if Bob had taken him back. The fact was that Gerald hadn't picked up his black marker since Tammi shot him the deuces.

Up until that moment, he had not believed in the possibility of writer's block. He had written the strip for three years, one each week, over 156 consecutive cartoons. He went from being ever-ready to being completely zonked. He wouldn't have been able to continue the strip at this point anyway, his brief lap into sycophancy not withstanding.

Being unemployed was not an option. He needed to figure out something new going forward.

Although Charlotte worked as a human resources manager, she didn't have much advice for how Gerald should proceed with his job search. The truth was Gerald hadn't held down a 9-to-5 job in quite some time and bristled at the idea of trying to frame his work life into a resume.

"Well, I guess it's good for you that we live in a 'gig' economy," Charlotte finally said.

"What does that mean?"

"Just look beyond the job sites for hustles you'd never find with a search engine."

Gerald considered this, but, honestly, didn't understand what the hell his sister meant.

His small, unimpressive efficiency had been paid up for the year, one of his smarter decisions. He also had a little tucked away in savings to last him a while. But there was the emptiness, the need to do something with himself that hammered away at him.

One of the things his late parents had instilled in his sister and him was that they needed to be doing something with their lives, even if it was unconventional.

His parents hadn't lived to see him become a cartoonist, but Charlotte had, and she'd been supportive, so that was all that mattered.

WITH NOTHING TO WRITE ABOUT, he found himself "people watching" from his third floor window. He wondered where they were going or where they were coming from and what they did for a living. He'd read somewhere that people were either coming out of hell, going into hell, or currently in hell when it came to their lives. He couldn't tell exactly what part of the equation he was in yet.

He did several sketches of the neighborhood from his window, just to keep his hand moving, but there was no story there. Just a bunch of random, disconnected images.

19

HE SPOTTED her from his window: an older woman adorned in a white rabbit coat. In the artsy part of town where Gerald lived, that was an egregious sin, yet he couldn't look away.

So he raced downstairs, and from the distance of at least a block, he followed her for roughly a quarter of a mile before she walked downward into a building, one that he'd walked past many times but had ignored due to its anonymity.

In the window was a small sign that read "You are here."

He descended the dark, narrow staircase and entered the building.

THE WOMAN in the fur coat was nowhere to be found, but Gerald found himself oddly curious about the shop in which he stood. There was barely any light in the room, save a small lamp on the counter near the register. The room was full of reams of paper and binders, yet nothing was for sale.

A small woman sat listlessly behind the counter, unable to keep her head from nodding off onto her outstretched arm.

"Excuse me," Gerald said. "What is this place?"

"It's a Brautigan library," the girl responded, without attempting to look up.

A Brautigan library?

The
Library
For
Tortured
Souls

"WE LIKE to call it the Library for Tortured Souls," the woman said, finally lifting her head. "We collect the incomplete manuscripts of writers who are unable to finish them."

Gerald shrugged his shoulders. "Do *you* finish them?"

"No. We store them. That way they can move on with their lives."

"Interesting."

"Not really," she responded. "But what *is* interesting is that we're hiring. You looking for a job?"

With a situation so oddly serendipitous, he naturally looked for cameras from a prank show. When he saw none, he asked, "What will I do and how much do you pay?"

THE INCOMPLETE BOOKS in the main area were nothing compared to the ones filed away in the back of the library. Gerald had no idea so many people had written chunks of books, only to abandon them and feel the need to take them away so that they didn't continue to obsess over them.

"Uno Pérez came here several times, but at the last minute he'd change his mind and take his book with him. Someone told me he ended up with a Pulitzer Prize for that one," she said, clearly irritated.

Gerald didn't want any parts of that conversation.

"Who was that woman in the fur coat?"

"Oh, that's The Queen. She drops off a manuscript every couple of weeks. Always leaves out through the back."

She must be really tortured if she starts and abandons manuscripts so often, Gerald mused.

"Sydney," the woman energetically offered, vigorously shaking his hand.

"Gerald," he responded.

"So you want a look at the application?" she said, comically waving a piece of pink paper back and forth.

"Can I ask how long you've been working here?" he said.

Sydney lifted her hand and began counting her fingers. Finally she stopped and said, "Forever."

GERALD TOOK THE JOB, not because he needed one that paid so little, but because he felt it was the kind of quirky arrangement that might unlock his creativity.

Most of his day was spent sitting around while Sydney slept on a cot in the back. She was studying for the bar exam and took frequent naps throughout her work shift. It didn't bother Gerald, though. He spent his time perusing some of the incomplete manuscripts, quickly discovering why many of them were cast aside.

Maybe one day the woman in the fur coat would return.

He certainly hoped so.

LATER THAT EVENING when Gerald called Charlotte, he had trouble explaining to her what the Library of Tortured Souls was and what exactly he did there.

In the end, she simply said, "It's a job, right?"

"Yes."

"All right then."

In their family, that was all that really mattered, according to their late parents. Idle hands were the devil's workshop, they all believed.

When he got off the phone, he picked up his black marker.

The well was still dry. Not a thought in his head.

He tried to draw Sydney sleeping on the counter or the cot, but failed.

"So you're a cartoonist?" Sydney asked, during one of the rare moments she was actually conscious.

"Yes. I had a comic strip for three years."

"Then what happened?"

"I proposed to my ex-girlfriend and she said no. After that I couldn't do my strip."

Sydney sighed. "Man, that must suck. Wait, you can still draw, though, right?"

"For the most part, I guess. Why?"

"I have a friend who is looking for someone with your talents."

"To do what?" Gerald responded.

"I think it's best I let *him* explain all of that to you. He is quite the character!"

"COME AGAIN?" Gerald said, looking the man over. He had roughly average height, average build, nothing exceptional about him other than his hazel eyes, which looked mysterious on a man of his bronze complexion.

"I want you to draw a caricature of my girl-friend and me fucking."

A million questions flooded Gerald's mind. *Why would they want a humorous drawing of such a serious act? Were they tired of using their smart phones?*

As he prepared to decline the offer, the man sweetened the deal. "I'll pay you $1,000—and if you make me *bigger*, I'll throw in another $250."

Even as Gerald rode the elevator to the fourth floor of the apartment building that Friday evening, he could only wonder how he'd found himself in this situation. Surely doing something this ridiculous would unlock his ability to write a strip.

The guy, Dexter, greeted him at the door, already in a terrycloth robe, as if he were a porn actor waiting to be called to the set.

He quickly introduced Gerald to his girlfriend, Naima, whose long beautiful locs were pulled into a ponytail. She, too, wore a robe.

"We didn't want to get started without you," Dexter said.

THEY CAME out of there clothes like they were extras in *The Wiz*, Evillene had just been killed, and he was about to see a "brand new day."

"Remember what I said about the tip," Dexter said, winking and taking his place on the edge of the bed.

Naima knelt down in front of him and went to work.

Gerald didn't know if he was supposed to be drawing the foreplay, so he did a quick sketch of her priming him and him priming her.

He thought he would've felt more uncomfortable than he did, but everything was just mechanical.

"THIS IS THE POSITION RIGHT HERE," Dexter said, standing up from the bed with Naima still straddling him. "Get this one!"

Gerald started drawing feverishly.

"Quick! 'Cause I'm about to bust!" Dexter yelled.

Not to quote Karen Carpenter, Gerald thought, but they'd only just begun. Definitely less than twenty pumps, and this guy was about to be done.

Gerald quickly sketched their faces, exaggerating them, along with their bodies (sure to secure his tip for the evening).

And like that, it was over.

The couple waited eagerly to see the finished product, their fingers interlocked.

Gerald didn't want to disappoint.

GERALD DIDN'T KNOW how to feel about the experience, but the couple was pleased (and he got his tip), so that was all that truly mattered.

On the way out the door, Dexter said, "Hey, I might have some more clients for you. Would you be interested?"

Thinking of the cash in his pocket, he said, "Sure. Why not?"

Leaving the apartment building, he realized that he had now picked up two strange gigs since he lost his syndication. He suddenly became curious about what the future held if he continued to say yes to the most unusual of things.

SYDNEY ASKED ABOUT THE SESSION, but quickly grew bored with Gerald's mundane details.

"He looks like he could really put it down," she said, lifting her reading glasses up onto her curly hair.

"Well, truthfully, it was like that Tootsie Roll commercial, with the 'how many licks does it take?' For him, it was about 20."

Sydney shook her head dismissively. "It's always the fine ones who can't fuck."

"I wouldn't know about that," Gerald said. "I've been ugly my whole life."

Sydney laughed so hard she snorted a little, and he suddenly wondered if she knew he was joking.

WHILE SITTING at his work desk, listening to Coltrane, he challenged himself to write a complete strip. He stared at the three blank panels, like he had many times before, but he couldn't see it. There was no setup, no punchline.

Then something strange happened.

He decided to just draw, as best he could from memory, Dexter and Naima, but rather than stop there, he put a speech bubble next to Dexter that said, "TMinus 3..." and a thought bubble next to Naima that said, "Doesn't the countdown start at 10?"

He looked at the cartoon and smiled.

One panel.

GERALD KNEW BETTER than to get excited. After all, there wasn't much ink in the well just yet. There was more life to live, more experiences to draw from.

Before reporting to the Library of Tortured Souls, he sketched a single panel of Sydney sitting at the front desk with comical toothpicks holding up her eyelids to keep them from closing. Beneath the strip, he wrote "Will work for caffeine."

It wasn't as funny, but it was something, and he had been drawing long enough to recognize inspiration in its various disguises.

Maybe Charlotte's "gig economy" idea had some merit.

"WHAT WILL you do after you pass the bar?" Gerald asked Sydney.

"Celebrate."

"Well, yeah. But what else?"

"You don't get it, Gerry. This is my eighth time taking the damn bar. I just want to pass it. I'll figure out the other stuff later. It's not like I have law firms knocking down the door to offer me a job."

In that moment, Sydney became the most interesting person he knew. He had a million questions as to how she found herself in this strange place, operating autonomously, as if the owner were just a figment of everyone's imagination.

"WHAT IS the most difficult part about studying for the bar?" Gerald asked.

"Just keeping my mind sharp for the duration of the test. At first I thought it was me, so I took Adderall. Didn't work. It's like my mind just disconnects during the two days of the exam."

"Maybe you should just do something else then."

"That's what I'm doing here. It's a job, but it leaves so much time to do other things. I figure studying for the bar is better than masturbating to stay awake."

Gerald simply nodded. It definitely wasn't the strangest thing he'd heard.

AFTER A MONTH of working at the Library of Tortured Souls and doing two other caricature sessions with some of Dexter's friends, Gerald began to grow restless. He could see how Sydney struggled to stay awake. There was something about working for hours in a dungeon of incomplete manuscripts that dulled the mind.

It was still a job, he reminded himself. But so was manually inseminating cows. Or mopping up vomit from the restroom floor of a night club. Or shoveling horse manure.

He missed his old job—all of it.

He just needed a plan to get it back.

GERALD'S ONE-PANEL cartoons were coming along slowly, but steadily. They were similar to *Broken Bicycle* in some ways, but popped a bit more. They were what would happen if *Broken Bicycle* married Larson's *The Far Side* or Knight's *(Th)ink*. He would need to practice until he felt that he could handle a steady commitment of content to a syndication company. Maybe he'd reach out to Bob again, but that situation went south in a way that felt personal, so maybe not. Plus, there were a number of other syndication companies out there. Maybe one of them would be interested.

JUST AS HIS Friday shift was coming to an end, in walked the woman in the fur coat! He hadn't noticed the movie star shades before, but her golden brown bun was pulled so tightly that her forehead was screaming her thoughts. There was something intriguing about her, though, even in her aloofness.

She walked to the counter, placed down what looked like no more than thirty pages and proceeded to walk out the back door.

"Excuse me, miss!" Gerald called out.

She stopped in her tracks, as if insulted that he'd spoken to her.

"What's your name?" he said.

SHE TURNED to face him and lifted her shades. Rather than speak, she simply winked.

For a moment, he stood there, stunned.

In the time it would take a sloth to cross a road, she lifted her hand to greet him. When he touched her fingers, a soothing electricity trickled up his fingertips into his body, as if she'd exhaled gently against the back of his neck.

"Lock up for me," he called back to Sydney, though he didn't know if she was awake.

The mystery woman continued toward the backdoor, and this time Gerald followed her without a word.

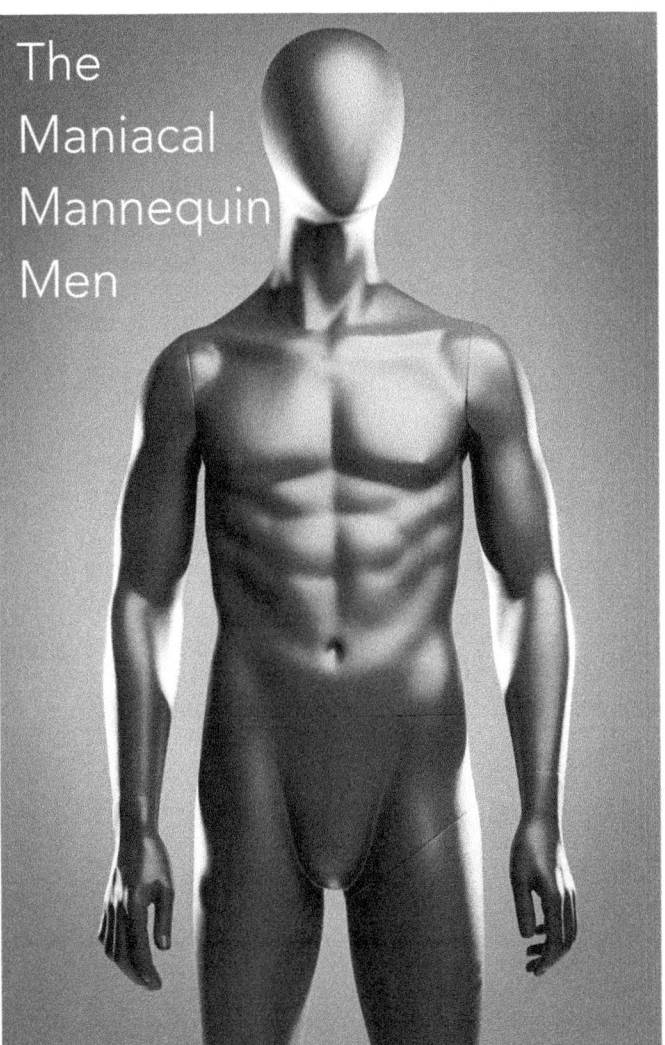

The
Maniacal
Mannequin
Men

THEY WALKED in silence for eight blocks, stopping at a building at the edge of a ritzy neighborhood and the art district. Even in the fall air, Gerald could feel the sweat dripping down his back beneath his relaxed oxford shirt, but he suspected there was not a drop of perspiration beneath the rabbit fur of the woman in front of him.

She turned around, smiled at him, then ascended the stairs into the building, Gerald in tow.

They took the elevator to the penthouse floor.

"You," she said, with a vague European accent, "stand over there with the others."

A GROUP of men of all shades and builds stood against the wall, many of them looking just as confused as Gerald felt.

She faced the group and lifted her shades. "Disrobe," she commanded.

Gerald could feel something in himself suddenly needing to be released from his clothing. He watched the others stripping down, and a calm settled over him as his fingers undid the buttons of his shirt.

Once he was nude, he looked around at the other naked men. They were all unremarkable, their bodies indistinguishable from another. In Gerald's mind they looked like crayons from a box.

THE WOMAN BECKONED FORTH the first of the naked men. She slowly circled him, like a sculptor examining a block of clay.

"Francis!" she called out.

Suddenly a small, impeccably dressed man appeared from seemingly nowhere.

"Bring me number 747, dear."

Francis disappeared and returned moments later with a purple cloak.

The woman swiftly wrapped it around the naked man, then stood back to examine the way the fabric rested upon his body.

She nodded carefully, considering what she saw.

"You," she said to the man, "stand on the other side of the room. Now."

Gerald patiently waited his turn.

THE TURQUOISE SILK cloak felt surprisingly good against his skin. Without a mirror, he could only affirm its appearance from the approving eyes of the woman.

He, too, was sent to join the other men on the opposite side of the room.

The woman then exited the room, Francis in tow.

When the men were alone, Gerald suspected someone would speak. When no one did, he tried to open his mouth, but found that he couldn't, nor could he produce a sound from his throat.

A part of him knew he should have been panicking, but he remained oddly calm.

As he stood there, his mind felt empty, as if he'd never been anything other than this "model" of sorts. Years earlier, he'd taken up Zen, but quickly found that his mind was too restless to maintain a sitting practice. The relaxation he'd been searching for then was now upon him, and the peace of it all made him want to stand in the same spot forever in an effort to maintain it.

The other men looked equally at peace. It was silently agreed they would not leave. No, they would wait, their silk cloaks caressing their bodies and minds.

SOME TIME later (no one was sure how long), the woman reappeared and ordered them to join her for dinner. They naturally formed a single-file line and walked the length of the apartment to a long table containing an array of fresh garden vegetables.

"Eat," she commanded, so the men reached for carrots, radishes, spinach, lettuce, onions, and cucumbers, biting into them whole.

It was the most incredible meal Gerald had ever tasted!

Once they finished, she had Francis escort them back into the original room down the hall, where they were to rest for the remainder of the evening.

THE NEXT MORNING the woman returned. Again, she stared at them individually before dressing them again, this time in silk robes where the hues bore more earth tones.

For lunch, she fed them more vegetables.

She did another change of clothes on them, then dinner.

Biting an onion, Gerald suddenly began to laugh.

One by one the other men began to laugh until the entire table, sans the woman, were doubled over, vegetable juices and pieces spewing from their mouths.

"Silence!" the woman said, and they obeyed.

They continued to eat, but Gerald could see something different in Francis's eyes.

During the night he heard the screams, anguished and scared, barely loud enough for anyone to hear. The urgency did little to affect the tranquility of Gerald's mood.

Then the screams grew louder until they ceased.

Gerald suddenly became aware of how awkward he felt. *What the hell was he wearing? Who the hell were all these dudes?*

Suddenly that Francis guy burst into the room in a blood-soaked three piece suit screaming, "The witch is dead! The witch is dead! Run!"

Gerald didn't know what that meant, but he knew he had to get the hell out of there.

WHEN THE NEWS later reported that a fashion designer had been slain in her loft, there was no mention of the thirty or so men who had fled the building in different directions, their bodies blending into the night like apparitions that dissipated upon sight.

Gerald, sitting in his efficiency, wrapped himself in an afghan, listening to Coltrane's "Favorite Things."

He could scarcely remember any details of what had happened.

He did, however, know that he wouldn't return to the Library of Tortured Souls. He couldn't bear the thought of seeing Sydney after all of this. What would he say?

THE NEXT MORNING Gerald reluctantly changed his mind. He still needed to pick up his last paycheck.

When he arrived at the store, though, the "You are here" sign was no longer there, and the door was locked.

He peered through the dusty film on the dark window, and he slowly realized that what he assumed was a dimly lit space was not lit at all. The place was completely dark. He could not make out the manuscripts or anything. There was no evidence of life.

Gerald returned home, wondering if the library had ever really been there at all.

Sitting at his drawing table, a large white sketching pad before him, he drew a single panel. In the panel he drew a long line of mannequins and a woman standing before them. In that moment he didn't know what or how to feel about any of it. It hadn't been the troubling scene he saw before himself—or at least it hadn't felt that way—until the end, when it seemed all of his senses had heightened to a feverish pitch.

He wondered where the other men were now that they'd returned to their regular lives.

What about Francis?

GERALD ALSO WONDERED about Sydney and what might have happened to the Library of Tortured Souls, where all of the manuscripts had gone, and, finally, if any of it had been real.

She seemed just as real as he, and there was a part of him that wanted to search for her online, but he trusted that wherever she was, she was either studying for the bar exam or sleeping. That idea comforted him.

He hadn't left his house in a week, except for occasional meals. His mind still needed to be cleared.

He suddenly wondered how Tammi was doing.

THE PANELS HAD BECOME DARKER in the weeks that followed, as he wrestled to find the funnier side of life. He'd once read that comedy and horror were two sides of the same coin. It's just now he was having trouble flipping the coin to the side that would evoke laughter.

The mannequin men continued to appear in his panels, with several of them featuring the men laughing at the dinner table as they ate vegetables. Maniacal, they were.

Were they really hypnotized? How had she selected each of them? What would have happened to them if they'd never left?

To RID himself of ideas of the Stepford men and the woman who masterminded it, Gerald busied himself by reading through the entirety of *Broken Bicycle* to prove to himself he could actually do something right.

About 100 strips in, he started to notice something: he had gone from simply telling about the light-hearted, superficial observations of life to really interrogating his life. Nothing seemed off limits. And Tammi was in most of them.

He had drawn the time she'd gotten laid off from work. He had drawn when her grandmother died of cancer.

Yes, he *had* gone too far.

IN HIS DEFENSE, he supposed, any good cartoonist should be able to address anguish, fear, and grief in a comic strip. Some of the classic *Peanuts* strips depicted the somber side of life. But that was Schultz's deft hand, not his own. Maybe he'd been coming up short the entire time and just didn't know it.

Even more, assuming he had occasionally hit that mark as a cartoonist, he had still been a shitty boyfriend.

Why had Tammi stayed with him for so long? He arrived at one simple conclusion: she had to build up the courage to finally leave.

"You NEED to go on vacation, little brother," Charlotte said.

Gerald lay on his bed, the phone on speakerphone next to him. "Where would I go? I don't even have any money to travel."

Charlotte was notorious for not loaning out money, and Gerald knew better than to ask.

"You need a *stay-cation*, where you stay at home and turn your city into a vacation spot. You know, see it through the eyes of a tourist."

The idea of wandering the streets of the city overwhelmed him. He wasn't one of those flâneur people, wandering for the sake of wandering.

GERALD THOUGHT he'd never see the man again, but there he was, standing at the counter in the bodega, paying for a bottle of Perrier. The guy's small stature was unmistakable, even in a hooded sweatshirt, a baseball cap, baggy jeans, and a pair of Air Jordan 12's.

It was Francis!

The last time he'd seen Francis, the guy was dressed in a three-piece suit and covered in blood. Now he was just a regular brother, *incognegro*.

Francis looked up and noticed Gerald.

Neither said a word.

Finally, Francis gave Gerald "the nod" and promptly disappeared into the neighborhood.

58

GERALD HAD BEEN WAITING for the right time to apologize to Tammi—for everything. He could have been better for her in every regard. She needed to know that.

Still, her last words to him were pretty final. She'd washed her hands of him just like Bob had, and he'd had to learn how to deal with that.

There was no going backward. He thought about Omar Khayyám's famous quote, "The pen having writ, moves on," and realized how true that was. The only way forward was to keep moving, even if he had no idea where he was going.

"So I KNOW you're going to the masquerade ball this year," Otis said, laughing thunderously through the phone.

It seemed like the only time Gerald ever heard from Otis was when there was some holiday party coming up. He wasn't even sure he could call Otis a real friend, as he was only reliable when it came to parties.

He'd forgotten about the masquerade ball—had even forgotten Halloween was approaching—but he knew he needed to do something fresh to help take his mind off of things and to help him get his groove back.

"Of course," he responded.

THE PARTY SEASON started with the Halloween masquerade ball, then went on to the Christmas party, and ended with the New Year's gala. This was the only time Gerald even talked to Otis. They had a purely seasonal friendship, but when the season was upon them, they were thick as thieves, talking hours a day, hanging out and shooting the shit, full-blown best friends until January 2nd, at which point they'd ghost each other again until around the second week of October, where the cycle would instinctively begin again.

Gerald didn't mind, though.

The season of Otis had finally arrived.

The
Season
of
Otis

OTIS WENT as the same character every year, with mild variations in the quality of each costume: a wombat.

The first time Gerald had asked about the costume, Otis had promptly responded, "When I was a shorty, I watched this show on PBS called The *Clyde Frog Show*. No one seems to remember it, though, so I go dressed as Clyde's favorite toy, a stuffed wombat, hoping people will remember."

"Why not go as Clyde Frog then?" Gerald responded.

"And get confused for Kermit or Pepe? Nah, son, I'm good."

After that, Gerald stopped asking questions and focused on himself.

SEVERAL YEARS back when Otis went to the masquerade, he'd gotten into an altercation with a dude. Otis had made his move on a beautiful woman dressed as a member of the Dora Milaje. They were hitting it off fabulously when her ex-boyfriend rolled up on them.

"I can't believe you!" the dude said to his ex. "You're gonna pick this big ass rat over me?"

Before she could respond, Otis yelled out, "I'm not a rat! I'm a wombat, motherfucker!" Then he pulled out a set of nunchucks from his marsupial pouch and proceed to beat that ass.

PART of the fun of hanging out with Otis was in his unpredictability. Gerald never knew what kind of adventures the two of them would get into together.

That first masquerade where they'd met, both of them had been holding up the wall, nursing drinks. They struck up a conversation, and emboldened by their friendship (and newly minted wingman statuses), they ended up going home with a set of cousins who were so freaky that Gerald and Otis had to spend three days recuperating.

Since then, they were like Wonder Twins (*activate!*) and refused to take on the circuit alone.

OTIS HAD MADE a few appearances in *Broken Bicycle*, and while the fans seemed to really like him as a character, Gerald only used him between October and January. Finally, Bob had told him to stop teasing this character and either make him full-time or stop using him so infrequently.

He opted to stop, much to Otis's chagrin.

"Right when a motherfucker is starting to get some recognition, you pull the plug on him," Otis had said—but only during the following season, which, by that point, it didn't really matter, so Gerald shrugged and took it in jest.

Even though Otis knew what his costume would be, he didn't know which wombat costume he would use. Gerald, on the other hand, had no clue what he would go as, his mind still a bit shaken by the mannequin incident, his time at the library, and his failed relationship.

The good thing about costumes, though, was that they allowed a person to become something else entirely different. He had social permission to act and present himself in a whole new way.

Suddenly, an image of Francis in street clothes crossed his mind.

You could disappear into a new reality.

"AND YOU KNOW WHAT? She was dancing around in a motherfucking wombat suit! Beautiful, I tell you."

Otis couldn't stop gushing over Tomi Adeyemi, his favorite author, dancing around in a svelte wombat costume on her Twitter feed.

"I didn't even know wombats could be sexy," he said, winded from his enthusiasm.

"The jury is still out on whether a wombat can be sexy, but I get where you're coming from," Gerald responded.

"I heard about a new costume shop downtown. You down?"

Shifting his phone in his hand, Gerald responded, "You already know."

"That's what's up. It's wombat time!"

THE SHOP WAS in a neighborhood a few blocks from Lattimore College, a place full of pizza and tattoo parlors and students leaning against buildings, vaping and philosophizing on the kind of minutia that extends from overpriced classes.

The place was like most of the costume shops they'd visited in years past, but there was a plethora of costumes.

Otis immediately homed in on a wombat costume in the back.

"Hey, maybe we could both be wombats," Gerald said.

Gerald could hear Otis's cheeks slapping against his teeth in the back of the store as he shook his head "no."

OTIS FELL in love with his wombat suit and didn't mind that he had to pay $400 for it!

Gerald had less commitment to the costume process, and, as usual, he was still looking for his costume well after Otis had finished.

He'd only been half-kidding about going as a wombat, but Otis wasn't having it.

What *did* you wear when your boy was going as a *wombat*?

Gerald would've gone as a clown, but Otis hated clowns. Gacy, Pennywise, and Twisty had done him in. He was Diddy-level scared of them.

Gerald couldn't bring himself to scare a wombat.

AFTER HOURS of circling the shop, Gerald finally decided on a costume: Frank the Bunny from *Donnie Darko*. The costume was significantly cheaper than Otis's, but still not free. For a person who was unemployed, that definitely mattered.

So it was settled. They'd go as a wombat and a demented bunny.

This year's masquerade ball was hosted by an African-American fraternity and would take place uptown at a classy club known for such soirees.

They were still a week out from the party, but the energy was starting to build to a feverish pitch.

Gerald needed this more than Otis.

RELIEVED TO finally have a fellow guy to talk to, Gerald told Otis all about how he lost his job, how he lost his girl, and how he found himself working for a place that didn't seem to exist, before being abducted by a fashionista hypnotist who was murdered.

Otis's response wasn't, "You've got to call the cops!" or "Have you received any therapy for this shit?" He just poked out his lips in a grimace, shrugged his shoulders, lifted his eyebrows and tilted his head to the side. "That's fucked up, dude."

"Yep," Gerald responded, as they pondered this.

OTIS WAS JUST as eager to fill Gerald in on his "goings ons." He was still working at the post office, but he'd made some progress with his rap career, recording sixteen bars for a Marz Banx track, even though it got cut out on the final version. "Still, it's progress," Otis said smiling. "The fact that I got to spit on a Marz track puts me in a different league."

Gerald agreed and was happy for his friend.

"Maybe you should do a rap about wombats," he joked.

"Don't tempt me, son," Otis said. "Them wombats is a beast!"

OTIS GOT word that the masquerade was being cancelled due to some unknown reason, the planners feeling no need to explain anything.

"But we spent money on these costumes! I don't have money to throw away!" Gerald said, trying unsuccessfully to push away his dread.

"We'll just find a different party. Let me ask around and see what's up," Otis responded.

Gerald had always relied on Otis to know where to go, but he figured since he'd once done it himself, he could do some looking, too.

"You should draw a strip about this."

Gerald smiled, realizing Otis was right.

73

"WE'RE GOING to the Poe Ball," Otis proclaimed.

"How much is it?"

"It's invitation only."

"And where do we get the invitations?"

"We don't," Otis said. "We're gonna crash that bitch."

"I'm not sure that's a good idea."

"If we get caught, we just play the 'ignorant' card. The worst they can say is no."

Gerald sensed that wasn't the worst that could happen, but he trusted Otis, probably more than he should've.

"So where's this party?"

"At some uptown loft."

Suddenly Gerald had thoughts of the fashionista.

"Dude, I can't go back there."

"Yes, you can. I'm with you."

GERALD WOKE up on Halloween so nervous he could hardly eat. Part of him wanted to bail on Otis, but Otis was his only real connection to the "real world" at this point, and he didn't want to lose it.

Later that evening as he donned his Donnie Darko duds, he wondered if he was just over-thinking things. Surely, they'd get stopped at the door and probably end up wandering around downtown pub crawling with other people in transition between parties. Maybe they'd find a spot to go that way.

His apartment buzzer rang.

"Yo, G, the wombat is here!"

EVEN FROM STREET LEVEL, Gerald and Otis could hear Pharoahe Monch's "Simon Says" rumbling through the concrete of the sidewalk.

"Fucking Godzilla, gotdammit!" Otis said, staring up at the building like it was the Stay-Puft Marshmallow Man. "We doing this?"

Gerald nodded.

They took the elevator with a group of zombies, one of them rapping the lyrics, as another looked on in embarrassment.

When the door opened, the music came at them in a tsunamigenic wave.

"I can't hear myself think," Gerald said.

"Just stay close," Otis yelled.

In the chaotic environment, they sneaked in behind the zombies, easily undetected.

AFTER A WHILE, either the music softened or Gerald grew used to it. Otis had already hooked up with one of the zombies from the elevator, but Gerald was still feeling his way out. The worst thing he could do was lean on the wall, so he decided to remain close to the dance floor.

When Biggie's "Mo Money Mo Problems" came on, a woman dressed as Babs Bunny eased up to him and started dancing. He leaned in closer to offer his name, but she stopped him.

"No names."

They danced the next five songs, never removing their masks.

THE DJ abruptly stopped the music and the lights came on. Confused, everyone stopped dancing, some of them glancing at their watches wondering if they'd missed something.

A guy dressed as Kermit the Frog took the microphone and removed his mask. It was Bob!

Bob walked over to a woman dressed as Miss Piggy and knelt down, a ring in his hand.

"Tammi Renee Stevens, will you do me the honor of being my wife?"

She quickly removed her mask and jumped up and down, responding, "Yes!"

"Who proposes at a party?" Babs said to Gerald.

"My ex-boss, that's who."

GERALD STOOD PARALYZED LOOKING at Bob and Tammi. So that's who swooped in and snatched her up. That explained so much, Gerald thought.

The lights went back out and the music came back on.

"Wanna dance?" Babs asked.

"Sure," Gerald responded, deflated.

"Don't sweat them. If she's hooking up with Pepe the Frog, then she wasn't worth your time anyway."

In spite of himself, Gerald laughed.

"Now put your back into it," Babs said, dancing low to the floor.

He squatted and tried his best, but fell back onto his ass.

They both laughed for the rest of the song.

"FOR ALL THE lovers in the house, especially the frog and the pig," the DJ announced, dropping Keith Sweat's "Make It Last Forever."

This time Gerald asked Babs to dance.

"I thought you'd never ask," she said, chuckling and wrapping her arms around his waist.

They swayed to the beat, and in that moment he felt like he'd known her forever.

"Can we take off these masks? I really want to see you and know you're real," Gerald said.

"Real? What? Do you think I'm a ghost?" Babs responded.

"Stranger things have happened," he admitted.

They danced a little closer.

NEAR MIDNIGHT, Babs told Gerald she had to leave.

"Long day tomorrow?" he asked.

"Just studying for the bar."

"Sydney?"

Babs jumped back. "Who are you?"

"It's Gerald!"

"Wow!"

Gerald quickly removed his mask, as did Sydney.

"I came back to the store and you were gone!"

"We got evicted for nonpayment of rent."

"What about all those manuscripts?"

"They're in storage."

This had to be fate.

"Can I get your number?" he said, handing her his phone.

She began to punch in her number. "You'll have to figure out the last two digits, if you're really serious about this."

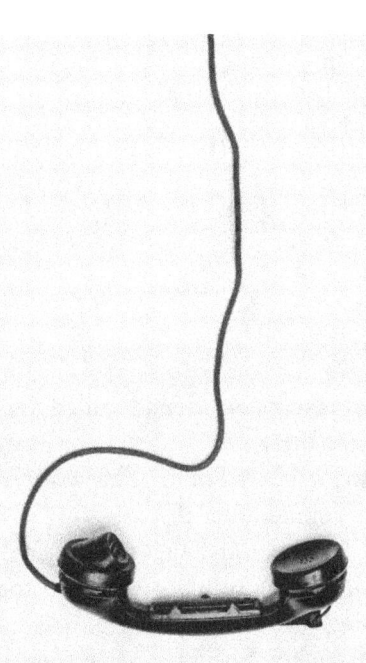

The
Denouement

THE NEXT AFTERNOON, Gerald called Otis and told him about Sydney.

"Two numbers?" Otis said. "That's like a gazillion numerical combinations!"

"It's 100," Gerald said, laughing.

"She's really going to make you earn that loving, I'm guessing."

"I can't blame her. She's a good person, and she wants to know I'm for real." He sighed. "Plus, she saw the whole proposal thing with Tammi. By the time I get through those combinations, I might be in a mental space to take her out."

"Hey, you do you," Otis said. "But check this: that zombie gave me Einstein-level brain last night."

THE NEXT PARTY would be Christmas, which felt like an eternity away. He and Otis would touch bases in a few weeks, just to keep the line of communication open.

In the meantime, Gerald was alone with only a sketch pad and a phone to keep him company.

He thought about Sydney and tried eight combinations, but he forgot to write them down, exhausted from the wrong numbers.

He picked up his black marker and drew a single panel. In it, he drew Tammi and Bob.

In this panel, Tammi said, "Yes!!!"

He balled it up and threw it away.

WHILE HE SHOULD HAVE LET it go and moved on, Gerald couldn't get over the odds of Tammi and Bob hooking up. At a certain point, things just weren't a coincidence.

He thought he would be more angry about it, but so much had happened since he and Tammi had broken up that he felt strangely detached from the news. Bob was still a rat bastard motherfucker, but that was largely beside the point.

They deserved each other, that was clear.

He wondered how he might've taken it if Sydney hadn't been there.

It felt like she'd always been there.

GERALD CREATED a chart for each of the numerical combinations so he could check them off one by one until he got to the right one.

Could he fall in love with a narcoleptic bar exam-flunking manager of an incomplete book repository?

Yes.

The real question, though, was could Sydney fall for an unemployed cartoonist with no friends, save his sister and a rapper who liked to dress up as a wombat?

That part remained to be seen.

Either way, he had to figure out the last two digits to get an answer to his question.

So he began (again).

Out of the blue, a letter arrived in the mail from Arroyo Syndications. At first Gerald thought they were reconsidering running *Broken Bicycle*, but the letter was a termination of contract and relinquishing of the rights for all of the *Broken Bicycle* strips. Gerald couldn't believe his good fortune. Maybe Bob had decided to do the right thing after all, at least with regard to Gerald's cartoon strip.

It wasn't a check exactly, but it was definitely the paper upon which a check could be written.

It was time to start querying publishers. Maybe someone'd want to publish the collection.

To KEEP himself busy while he awaited responses from different publishing houses, he worked on two one-panel cartoons each day. During his breaks, he would try out at least ten combinations of numbers.

By the end of the week, he was two-thirds through the list, and he had begun to wonder what he would say to Sydney when they finally talked. It had all been so natural at the Halloween party, but, in the larger scheme of themes, it had always been natural.

Sydney was both real and surreal, and he couldn't wait to get to know her better.

LATE SATURDAY AFTERNOON, after trying out the 86th numeric combination, she picked up.

"Hello?"

"Hi, may I speak to Sydney?"

"This is she."

Gerald closed his eyes and sighed. This was it.

"This is Gerald."

She yelled with excitement, as if she'd just found out she won the Publishers Clearing House sweepstake. He could hear her yelling away from the phone to someone else. "It's him! He called, girl!" Then she returned to the phone, and in a nonplussed voice said, "Nice of you to call."

He smiled so big that his cheeks began to ache.

He'd finally found her.

"I'm sorry," was the first thing Gerald could think to say. He'd left during his shift and followed a mysterious woman out of the library the last time he was around Sydney. Or maybe she'd been asleep and hadn't noticed.

"I was studying for the bar, and I looked up and you were gone."

They both knew this was a lie, but it was a convenient lie for both of them, so they let it stand in for the truth.

"Well, we found each other. That's all that matters."

"Agreed. So what's up?"

"You are. Are you free right now?

THEY MET at a coffee shop on the upper west side of the city. He figured the caffeine might come in handy, just in case she got drowsy.

They sat outside under a patio umbrella, the sun beginning to set behind them.

They talked and laughed, even questioning why neither had expressed interest in the other up until this point.

"There was that time when you said you'd been ugly your whole life, after I said fine brothers couldn't fuck."

"Oh yeah."

"But you're not ugly, so I hope that doesn't take away from the other part of the equation."

GERALD HAD ALWAYS HEARD of "petite mort," but to him it was just a sexual urban legend. But Sydney laid him out like Mike Tyson with a left hook. The bliss was so intense he lost consciousness for a minute, quite an irony as he was the one in their coupling that had the most experience staying awake.

"I guess I don't have to ask you how it was," Sydney said with a laugh.

He loved the fact that she didn't beat around the bush. It was refreshing to be with someone so open, so honest.

She gently kissed him.

THEY SPENT the weekend snuggled up in his apartment, and never once did they stop to ask where all of this was headed. Gerald was open to all possibilities, but he didn't want to push his luck. He had no other irons in the fire, nor any desire to be with anyone else, but he wasn't ready to ask Sydney the same question. He'd learned that it was best to live in the moment until there was no moment.

"I'm so glad you found me," she finally said.

"I am, too."

They kissed each other's bodies and fell asleep, together.

MONDAY MORNING, Gerald was awakened to a phone call from an unfamiliar number.

"Is this Gerald?"

"This is he."

"This is Memphis Wilkes over at Warehouse Press. You sent me a query for your compilation of *Broken Bicycle*."

"Oh, yes."

"I've been a fan since you started. Frankly, I'm surprised Arroyo let you go, but we would be interested in talking about publishing a collection of your work."

"That's fantastic!"

"We also have a syndication department for cartoons. Are you still doing the strip?"

"No—but I have something different, something better!"

"Better?" Memphis responded. "Well, let's talk about it."

GERALD'S APARTMENT felt different now. All of the so-so energy Tammi had brought to the place had evaporated. It was actually rather odd how quickly it occurred. Gerald felt absolutely nothing when he thought about her. All he could visualize was her in a Miss Piggy costume saying yes to Bob. Clearly, they were made for each other, so who was he to interfere with fate.

Plus, his nose was wide open with Sydney, who, as it turned out, didn't have narcolepsy after all and *was* legitimately tired from studying for the bar.

Hopefully she'd pass it this time around.

THE PRINCIPAL of MLK Middle School reached out to Gerald, again.

"We were wondering if you would come and speak to our students again next semester."

"It didn't really go so well last time, though. You sure you want me back?"

"The kids loved you! They think you're hilarious."

Gerald laughed. "Well, I can probably come back then."

"Just no more mama jokes," the principal said, laughing himself.

"No problem. I've given up cracking on low hanging fruit."

The principal laughed again, this time snorting. "Sorry about that."

"It's cool," Gerald responded.

Maybe things really were changing for the better.

BACK DURING GERALD's stint at the Library of Tortured Souls, he had read through several of the incomplete manuscripts of the woman Sydney had referred to as The Queen, the woman who'd been a mind-controlling fashion designer with a stable of hypnotized men, the woman who wrote under the name Iracebeth Bonham Crims, a name so scarily on the spot it gave him chills.

All of the stories were attempts at a Victorian tale involving a widowed queen trying to fight loneliness through a stable of male concubines.

His mind was never given a chance to make the connection, though.

"So HOW ARE things with you and Sydney?" Otis asked, as they sat down to lunch in midtown.

"Pretty damn good. You never realize what you were missing out on until someone comes along and opens up the world for you."

"Good for you. So you're going to write about her then?"

"Nope. I've learned my lesson. I don't want to share her with the world."

"Young grasshopper, I have taught you well."

They laughed.

"What about you and the zombie from the party?" Gerald asked.

"I got her number but never called."

"Why not?"

"I'm not built that way."

"You better be here for Thanksgiving," Charlotte said. "CMB, Gerald."

"Yeah, I know. 'We all we got,'" he said, quoting the famous line from the movie *New Jack City*. "I'll be there, but is it cool for me to bring someone with me?"

"Don't tell me you're back with Tammi."

"No. I have a new girlfriend. Her name's Sydney. She's good people."

"Sure. I'd love to meet her. And Gerald," Charlotte said, "don't take this the wrong way, but I wasn't too fond of Tammi. She didn't really seem that into you."

"I wish you'd've told me."

"No you don't."

"Okay," Memphis said. "I'm sending you a contract this week for the *Broken Bicycle* compendium. Have your lawyer look it over and get it back to me when you can."

"No problem."

"Also, Ted Jackson from the syndication side will be reaching out to you soon about your new one-panel cartoon. What are you calling it?"

"Black Marker."

"Catchy. I like that."

"Well, I'll be in touch. I'm really happy to be working with you. Did I mention I'm a fan of your work?"

"Yes, but I don't mind hearing it again," Gerald said.

"Talk to you later."

"A'ight. Peace."

"Baby, you're not going to believe this," Sydney said. "I have a job lined up for when I pass the bar! It's a small firm, just two lawyers, but it's personal injury, so I get a cut of the cases I close. Now I just have to pass the bar."

"You can do it. This is your time. You got this."

"I know you're just going through all of the supportive phrases you can, but I love you for it."

"I love you, too."

"It feels good to not be the thong stuck in someone's crack."

"Hey, don't I know."

"You think Charlotte'll like me?"

"Definitely," Gerald responded. "It's a fine time to ask, though."

"Yeah, it might've been good to ask before we got on this plane."

"She'll love you because I love you."

Sydney nestled her head against his shoulder. "I've never been to the west coast before."

"Trust me. You'll love it."

For a while they sat, enjoying the subtle humming of the plane around them. Gerald couldn't wait to introduce his two favorite people to each other.

Sydney suddenly whispered, "Did you ever hear about what happened to The Queen?"

"*No.* Can't say that I have."

ACKNOWLEDGMENTS

Special thanks to Elle and Zoë Walker, who make it possible for me to write. Also, thanks to Torrey Holbrook Walker, Sabin Prentis, Van G. Garrett, Chris L. Butler, and Scott Semegran for their support and encouragement on this project.

ALSO BY RAN WALKER

ABOUT THE AUTHOR

Ran Walker is the author of twenty-six books. He is the winner of the Indie Author Project's 2019 Indie Author of the Year Award, the 2019 Black Caucus of the ALA Fiction Ebook Award, the 2018 Virginia Author Project Award for Adult Fiction, and the 2021 Blind Corner Afrofuturism Microfiction Award. He teaches creative writing at Hampton University and at Writer's Digest University and lives with his wife and daughter in Virginia. He can be reached via his website, www.ranwalker.com.

www.ingramcontent.com/pod-product-compliance
Lightning Source LLC
Chambersburg PA
CBHW070312120726
47910CB00007B/2457